This book belongs to:

....

FOR THE TWO STALLIONS WHO MAKE MY LIFE 20% COOLER: GARETH AND JM

EGMONT
We bring stories to life

First published in 2013 in the United States by Little, Brown and Company
This edition published in 2019 by Egmont UK Limited The Yellow Building,
1 Nicholas Road, London W11 4AN

www.egmont.co.uk

Licensed by:

www.mylittlepony.com

978 1 4052 9499 7

70534/001

Printed and bound in Great Britain by CPI Group

Stay safe online. Egmont is not responsible for
content hosted by third parties.

MIX
Paper from
responsible sources
FSC® C020471

My Little Pony

Rainbow Dash
and the Double Dare

WRITTEN BY G. M. BERROW

Contents

* ★ ★ ★ *

CHAPTER 1
The Latest and Greatest

It was almost midnight in Ponyville, but nopony was tucked into bed yet. They all had the same good reason for staying up past their bedtime: there were only four minutes to go until it was *time*. Time for the most epic adventure ever to be released – *Daring Do and the Volcano of Destiny*!

'Omigosh, omigosh, omigosh!' said Rainbow Dash, a blue Pegasus pony with a rainbow-coloured mane. She began to pace around the patch of grass outside the Ponyville bookshop. Even though she would have the book in her hooves in less time than it took for her friend Pinkie Pie to throw together a party (her current record is four minutes, seventeen seconds), Rainbow Dash still felt so fizzy with anticipation that she thought she might explode. As awesome as a rainbow firework would look, however, she didn't have time for it. Not on the release night of the most incredible adventure book *ever*! Plus, if she exploded, she'd lose her place in line.

Three more minutes, she thought. Hardly any time at all! Yet it seemed like an eternity.

'Can't you ponies hurry it up in there?!' Rainbow whined as she peered through the bookshop window. The light was on and there was some movement inside, but the CLOSED sign had not been flipped around to OPEN just yet. Giant posters of Daring Do adorned the shop windows. They showed the famous adventurer Pegasus wearing her signature outfit – a khaki helmet and an olive green shirt. On the new book cover she was shown standing at a volcano bubbling with fiery red lava. The words above bore the book's title: *Daring Do and the Volcano of Destiny*. Below the cover, the poster read **MIDNIGHT RELEASE PARTY! GET YOUR COPY BEFORE EVERYPONY ELSE!**

Rainbow glanced at the large crowd behind her. It looked like two hundred ponies were there. Thank Celestia, she was first in line! Nopony else loved Daring Do as much as Rainbow Dash did. To prove it, she'd been camping out since the morning. She had brought all of the Daring Do books with her and had spent the day rereading them. When midnight struck, she wouldn't have to wait a single tick of the clock longer to find out what happened to Daring next.

The Daring Do series of books had become extremely popular lately, and Rainbow Dash suspected it was mostly because of her. She was a major trend-setter in Ponyville. Other ponies looked to her for anything awesome. So it was only natural that the bookshop had decided to make it a special event. Some of the ponies in line wore Daring Do costumes, and some munched on goodies from Applejack's treat cart. But they all had one thing in common – they were beyond excited to continue reading about Daring Do and her thrilling adventures.

'Get yer Apple Fritters... of Destiny!' Applejack said, trotting up and down the

line with a tray of treats for sale. 'Fresh Caramel Apples... of Doom!'

'Hey, Applejack?'

Rainbow asked her friend. They just looked like normal treats to her. 'Uh... what are you doing?'

'Figured I'd try to make my treats sound as Daring Do as I could,' Applejack explained. She passed a mini apple pie to Rainbow. 'Apple Pie of Fate?'

'Thanks, but no,' Rainbow said, pushing the treat away. 'It's almost time!'

Plot Twist, the yellow Earth pony with an orange mane who owned the bookshop, poked her head out of the door to count the ponies in line. 'So many readers!' she observed with delight.

'We're almost ready, everypony!' Plot Twist shouted. She was glad she had recruited Pinkie Pie to help her with the party. They had expected a large crowd, but nothing like this.

'Oh, man!' Rainbow squirmed. 'This is

taking forever!'

'Hiya, Rainbow Dash!'
Pinkie Pie chirped,
poking her fuchsia
mane out of the
window. 'Are you,
like, so totally excited
that you feel like

you're going to burst into a rainbow
firework of happiness now that
you're going to get the new Daring Do
book first?!'

'Exactly!' Rainbow nodded. 'Now, can
we get this show on the road? I have
a story to read! I have to know what
happens with Dr Caballeron! Is the
Volcano of Destiny his secret lair? Or
is it a decoy to distract Daring from
finding the Secret Stables of
Crickhowell?' With each word, Rainbow

inched closer to Pinkie's face like she was interrogating her.

Pinkie shrugged and smiled wide. 'I don't know, but it won't be long before you do! We're just putting the finishing touches to the replica of Ahuizotl's temple we made. It's built completely from books! Isn't that totally readeriffic?!'

'Yeah, yeah. Very cool. But hurry it up!' Rainbow said, jogging in place. She'd been outside for a long time. Her legs and wings were starting to cramp up. And since she'd been waiting alone, she hadn't had one chance for a flying break.

Rainbow had tried to get her friends to come, but none of them had wanted to wait all day long. Fluttershy and Rarity had stopped to visit but had to go and tend to some newborn goats and finish sewing hats for them. Twilight Sparkle loved Daring Do, too, but she had decided to wait until her copy arrived in the post the next morning. She mumbled some nonsense about needing sleep.

It was so silly! What could be more important than this?!

'Only one minute left, everypony!' Rainbow Dash shouted to the line. Her call was met with cheers. The sound of the crowd triggered something inside of her. It was more than enough time to make a grand entrance into the bookshop! If she flew at the door at just the right angle... yeah, she could do this. She would do it for Daring Do!

Rainbow Dash

turned to Applejack's big brother, Big McIntosh, who was behind her. He was wearing a Daring Do helmet and chewing on a piece of hay. She'd have to trust him to keep her place. 'Watch my spot, Big Mac!' she shouted.

'Eeeyup,' he said, nodding his light orange mane.

'Hey, Daring Do fans! Watch *THIS*!' Rainbow hollered. The ponies all started chattering. What crazy thing was Rainbow Dash going to do now? The store was about to open!

Rainbow bolted into the air, beating her blue wings as hard as she could. She

shot off, a rainbow trailing behind her
that was so bright it was visible in the
night sky. If a pony had blinked they
would have missed it.

'Hey, where'd she go?' asked Apple
Bloom, pointing to the sky.

'There she is!' squeaked Sweetie Belle.
'She's headed straight for the door!'

Up in the sky, Rainbow Dash could see
the sign on the door flip from CLOSED to
OPEN. The door was still closed, but if
she'd calculated the timing correctly,
everything would work out perfectly.
She'd be the first to get the book and
she'd do it with style.

'Here I coooooome!' Rainbow shouted as she completed a perfect triple barrel roll across the sky, leaving a corkscrew rainbow in her wake. Rainbow Dash swooped down. Everypony in line held their breath. Would she crash into the door? Apple Bloom and Sweetie Belle shielded their eyes with their hooves.

The ponies gasped as Rainbow hurtled forward, about to make contact. Then, at the very last second, the door opened!

'Iiiiincomiiiiiiing!' Rainbow yelled as she dived through, narrowly missing Plot Twist, who had come to greet the fans.

Bang! Boom! Crash!

All that was left of the grand towering replica of Ahuizotl's temple was a big pile of books with a rainbow Pegasus in the middle. Even though Rainbow's stunt had ruined the display, it was a good thing the books had been there to soften the landing. At least that's what Rainbow told herself as she looked around at the destruction. Sometimes it took a little sacrifice to do something impressive, so the trade-off was worth it. Plot Twist frowned. Clearly she didn't agree.

'My display is ruined!' Plot Twist cried, throwing her hooves in the air.

Rainbow gave a weak laugh as she

stood up, books falling off her. 'Whoops, sorry about that.' Then Rainbow snatched up a book, dropped her bits on the counter, and took off for Cloudsdale to read through the night.

CHAPTER 2
Patience is an Issue

'What about the part where Daring swooped through the barricade the henchponies had made?! I couldn't believe she made it! Even though they were blocking the path to the secret stone that unlocked the hidden gates that led to the road to the Volcano of Destiny!'

Rainbow Dash yelled.

Her voice was so loud that anypony within a mile radius of Ponyville Park could have heard her.

'Spoiler alert! La, la, la...!' Twilight sang as she held her hooves over her ears.

'Uh, Twilight? What are you doing?' asked Rainbow Dash, raising an eyebrow. 'Don't you want to talk about how amazing the book is?! Especially the part where—?'

'No!' Twilight yelled. She softened her tone and added, 'Sorry. I mean, no. No spoilers, *please*?'

'You're not finished yet?!' Rainbow whined, doing a dramatic twirl before falling to the ground. 'This is the worst!

I thought *you* of all the ponies in Equestria would be done reading it by now! Don't eggheads like you just, like, *look* at books and absorb what's in them, anyway?'

Twilight smirked. Sometimes Rainbow said things that sounded harsh but were compliments in disguise. When she called Twilight an *egghead*, she really meant that she thought Twilight was smart.

'Well, I *can* speed-read, but this is a book I want to enjoy.' Twilight held up her copy. 'A new one of these doesn't come out every day, you know.'

Of course Rainbow knew! She'd only been waiting for this Daring Do adventure for what – *months*?

'Hey! What is that and why didn't I get one?' She pointed to the Daring Do bookmark stuck between the pages. It was shaped like the famous relic from the first book in the series, *The Sapphire Stone*.

'They sell them at the bookshop. You can have this one if you want,' offered Twilight. She kindly passed it to Rainbow.

'Nah, it's OK,' Rainbow said, handing back the bookmark. It was a nice gesture, but Rainbow Dash's number one problem still wasn't solved. She needed to find somepony who had finished reading the book so she could go over all the new stuff that had happened in the story! 'How am I supposed to talk about the coolest parts of the story if nopony has finished it yet?' Rainbow groaned.

'Sorry, Rainbow,' Twilight said, taking a seat on her favourite bench on the edge of Ponyville Park. 'But I'm going to take my time.' She opened her book and got settled for a slow, relaxed reading session.

'I guess reading is just another thing that shows how fast I am and how slow everypony else is,' Rainbow Dash mumbled before taking off into the clouds. 'Story of my life.'

Fluttershy, who was leading a group of ducklings to the pond, happened to walk past just then.

Fluttershy noticed the look of dismay on Twilight Sparkle's face, so she made a detour. 'Hold it right there, little sweeties,' the yellow Pegasus cooed to her feathered followers. 'I'll be just an itty-bitty moment, and then we'll go for that paddle like I promised.' The ducklings responded with happy quacks.

'Hi, Fluttershy,' Twilight said, still

looking at the sky in concern. Up in the sky, Rainbow kicked a cloud in frustration. It disappeared with a poof. She looked for another puffy cumulus to take her anger out on.

'Is something wrong with Rainbow Dash?' Fluttershy asked. 'She seems... a little down.'

'She wants to talk about the new Daring Do book, but nopony's finished reading it yet,' explained Twilight.

'Oh, I just started reading it,' said Fluttershy. 'But I had to put it down to take care of my duckling duties. It's good so far!'

'I wish there was something we could do to help her. It's great to see a pony so excited about reading.' Twilight sighed. 'If I had it my way, everypony would read all the time! Then, we'd have meetings and exchange ideas.'

'So why don't you do that?' asked Fluttershy. 'It seems like fun!'

'That's perfect!' Twilight replied. 'We'll plan a Daring Do book club, and we can hold it at the library. Then Rainbow can talk about the books all she wants!'

Rainbow flew down so fast that Fluttershy and Twilight didn't even see her coming. 'Now THAT'S what I'm talking about!' she cheered as she did a backflip. 'By the way, I was totally listening to your whole conversation.'

CHAPTER 3
The Golden Oak Library Society

A few unbearably long days later, Rainbow Dash's wish was about to come true. Book Club Night! They would be talking about Daring Do all evening! By the time Rainbow arrived, Twilight

Sparkle's home was already bursting at the branches with ponies who had recently finished reading *Daring Do and the Volcano of Destiny*. Everypony had come prepared for the very first meeting of the Golden Oak Library Society. One by one, they filed into the library clutching their copies of the book. Rainbow Dash took a seat at the front and watched the room fill up. This was going to be awesome.

Plot Twist and Berry Punch walked in, followed by Lyra Heartstrings, Sweetie Drops and Wild Fire. They poured themselves cups of juice from Applejack's refreshments table and took their seats.

'Daring Do is such an exciting hero! I just love her!' said Berry Punch.

'This was the best book yet!' said Plot Twist. 'We sold out in the first hour.'

Sweetie Drops nodded. 'The next book

release will have to be even bigger.'

'Totally,' Wild Fire added, her voice monotone. The brown-maned pony wore a chilled-out expression. It was still the most excited she had ever looked.

Pinkie Pie popped up out of nowhere. 'Name tags, anypony?!' She passed each attendee a little red sticker that said: HELLO, I'M … _____. Pinkie was already wearing one, except instead of her own name, she'd written HELLO, I'M … <u>EXCITED</u>!

'You're *Excited*?' asked Sweetie Drops. The pony scratched her blue-and-pink mane in confusion.

'Sure am!' Pinkie replied. 'Aren't you?'

'I'm confused,' Sweetie Drops replied.

She already knew Pinkie Pie. 'You're—'

'And I'm excited you're here, *Confused*!' said Pinkie, passing her and Lyra some name tags.

'Sorry I'm late, darlings! I wasn't sure what one wears to a library society,' announced Rarity, waltzing in the door. She was decked out in a sweater over a  collared shirt and was wearing glasses. Her saddlebag was filled with quills and notebooks. She could have passed for a student at Mythica University. 'I never tried the bookish look, but I think it works on me, no?'

'You look great, Rarity!' said Spike, popping his head out from the other room.

Before Rainbow Dash could comment on Rarity's look, Fluttershy stepped inside. A little green inchworm followed her. He was wearing glasses and a tiny Daring Do pith helmet.

'I hope it's okay that I brought my friend William Wormsworth,' she said in her gentle tone. 'He's a bookworm. He begged to come along.'

William scooted to the top of a stack of Daring Do books.

'Of course,' said Rainbow anxiously. 'And it's nice to meet you, Will. But please sit down now so we can get on with it!' It felt like everypony moved slow on purpose to frustrate her!

But still, Rainbow was happy to see that all her friends had shown up. She was going to impress everypony with her new theory. Rainbow was sure that the

Volcano of Destiny would become the Hollow Hideout of the Stalwart Stallion of Neighples in the next book. Surely nopony else had made the connection between the newly recovered ancient map of the underground fortress of Mount Vehoovius in chapter four and its similarity to the one in *Daring Do and the Griffon's Goblet*. It had to be the same one!

'All right, everypony. Find a seat and we'll get started!' Twilight announced.

Twilight had worked hard to make the event official. The room was arranged so that the ponies could sit in a  semicircle. It was a bit like a classroom but more casual. The book-lined walls of the hollowed-out tree set the mood nicely. A chalkboard listed the order of business.

'Welcome!' Twilight chirped. 'I'm so glad you're all here to share in the joy of reading with me! In my opinion, there are not enough events in Equestria purely for celebrating books, especially the Daring Do series!'

For once, Rainbow Dash wholeheartedly agreed.

CHAPTER 4
The Double Dare

Pinkie Pie squirmed in her seat next to Rainbow Dash.

'Oh my goodness, Rainbow! You must be so thrilled! Daring Do is, like, your favouritest pony character ever, and we're about to spend *hours* talking about her! What are you thinking right now? What

are you feeeeeeling?' Pinkie leaned in close to Rainbow's face.

'I'm thinking I want to talk about Daring Do and I'm feeling annoyed that we aren't yet,' Rainbow deadpanned.

'OK, that's great.' Pinkie scribbled something on a notepad. 'And how does *that* make you feel?' She propped her chin on her hoof.

'Pinkie Pie!' scolded Twilight. 'We're starting! Shhhh.'

'Consider my lips zippified!' Pinkie magicked a zip out of thin air and taped it to her mouth.

'So...' Twilight motioned to her blackboard, which was filled with writing and diagrams. 'I've done some extensive research into how to run a book club meeting,' she explained. 'Number one on the agenda should be introductions of each member of the group.'

'I think we all know each other!' Rainbow shot back. 'Moving on!'

'Nuh-uh!' said Pinkie Pie, the zip falling off her mouth. She pointed to Sweetie Drops. 'Have you all met *Confused* yet?!'

Sweetie Drops shook her head in defeat.

Twilight ignored the exchange. 'OK, so if we skip that...next should be a quick recap of each chapter to refresh everypony's memory. Then, we'll move on to general interpretations of the text and its meaning, and last we'll go through the list of questions. We'll have one ten-minute snack break in the middle, so please visit Applejack's treat table then.'

Rainbow Dash looked around the room. She wasn't the only one who didn't think Twilight's schedule sounded all that fun. Rarity was busy inspecting her new hooficure, Sweetie Drops was staring out of the window, and Lyra Heartstrings was slouching down in her chair with her hind hooves dangling in front of her.

Rainbow jumped in before things got worse. 'I think I speak for everypony here when I say we can cut straight to discussing the action sequences.'

Plot Twist nodded her orange mane in agreement.

Twilight looked pretty disappointed that nopony liked her Library Society agenda.

Fluttershy felt bad. She raised a hoof and said, 'Twilight, if it's OK with you, William Wormsworth and I would love to stay after and discuss all your talking points. He usually has a lot to say, the little chatterbox!'

William sat on his chair, smiling but not saying a peep. He hadn't said a single word yet. He tipped his helmet to Twilight like a gentleman.

'It's all right,' Twilight sighed. 'Rainbow Dash, maybe you should take over.' Twilight found an empty seat.

Rainbow jumped up. 'First things first: I can't believe that move Daring Do did where she hitched a ride on the back of that dragon and let go right when she was over Ahuizotl's encampment! I can't wait to try that out sometime! Of course, I'll need help finding a dragon...'

'At your service!' said Spike proudly. It was silly because he was still just a baby – and far too small to pull off a stunt like that.

'Riiight.' Rainbow clapped her hooves together. 'Anywaaaay, how about I tell you all my amazing theory on the ancient map of Mount Vehoovius?!' This was her moment to wow them. 'So, you know how in book two – on page one hundred and sixty-three, to be precise – Daring Do is looking for the griffon's goblet when she happens upon a tablet that refers to an ancient map? I think that –'

Wild Fire raised her hoof, interrupting

Rainbow's flow. 'Um, excuse me?'

'Yeah?' Rainbow replied, trying to hide her annoyance. She didn't like being interrupted. Especially when she was about to say something so epic that it was going to blow everypony's minds.

'I like Daring Do as much as the next pony, but do you *really* think that all those daring things she does are *realistic*?' Wild Fire flipped through her copy of the book, frowning. 'No way could a pony ever really do them in real life!'

'She has a point,' said Lyra. She bobbed her mint green mane.

'Some of it is pretty far-fetched,' added a blue Unicorn seated in the back. A couple of other ponies murmured and nodded in agreement.

'Like the part where her wing injury is acting up, so she has to step out onto an invisible rope bridge to cross the canyon?' said Sweetie Drops, flipping to the page in her book. 'No way would anypony risk that.'

They were clearly missing the point of a fun adventure story. Twilight chimed in with a serious point. 'I don't think the purpose of the books is to –'

'Are you guys kidding me?!' Rainbow shrieked. Her eyes grew as wide as a couple of Granny Smith's prized giant zap apples. 'Of course all the stuff she does could be real! Daring Do is the bravest pony ever. I wouldn't be surprised if she *were* real!' Rainbow puffed up with pride.

Twilight, Applejack, Rarity, Fluttershy and Pinkie Pie each shot Rainbow a warning look.

'I guess I'd just have to see it to

believe it, is all,' Wild Fire said, giving a little shrug.

'Well ... maybe you can,' Rainbow Dash said, walking up to Wild Fire. The expression on Rainbow's face was a familiar one – determination. She'd looked the same when she saved Rarity by performing a Double Rainboom in the Cloudsdale Best Young

Flyer competition. Just like nothing would have got in the way of saving her friend from falling then, nothing was going to stop her from proving her point now.

'Oh yeah?' replied Wild Fire, standing up to challenge her. 'And just how are you going to do that?'

Applejack stood up and positioned herself between the two ponies. 'All right now, everypony, why don't y'all just slow yer trot for a second? This is a book club.'

'Oooooh, I sense a dare coming on! This meeting is much more exciting than I expected it to be!' Pinkie Pie said, jumping up and down. 'And I was already excited.' She pointed to her name tag. 'See?'

Rainbow turned to the rest of the ponies in the room. She climbed on top of a chair for dramatic effect. 'I ... I *dare* anypony here to dare me to do anything Daring Do could do!' She put her hooves on her hips in triumph.

'And I ... dare you to do so!' replied

Wild Fire. She narrowed her eyes. 'No –
I *double* dare you!'

Everypony gasped. To Rainbow Dash,
a dare was unbreakable. But a double
dare? That was a whole new crate of
apples.

CHAPTER 5
The Daring Dash-board

The next day, there was a big stir in the
Ponyville town square. Everypony was
gathered there. Pinkie Pie had taken the
lead in helping Rainbow Dash carry out
her dares.

Pinkie Pie stood proudly next to a
giant rainbow-coloured scoreboard,
making grand motions with her hooves

and urging ponies to write their challenges on it. The frame was surrounded in glittery clouds made of cotton balls and said DARING DASH-BOARD at the top. The proud expressions

on the faces of the Cutie Mark Crusaders – Apple Bloom, Scootaloo and Sweetie Belle – were dead giveaways as to who had helped make it.

Rainbow Dash trotted up and waited for the ponies to start showering her with words of praise. But they were all so busy admiring the Dash-board that they hadn't even noticed the guest of honour

had arrived! Rainbow
cleared her throat.
'Umm, guys? Bravest
pony in Ponyville present.
You can all chill out now,
because I'm here.'

'Oh wow, it's Rainbow Dash!'
shouted a small green Unicorn filly. 'Is
she really going to do whatever anypony
dares her to do?'

'She's here!' shouted Scootaloo,
Rainbow Dash's number one fan. A
rainbow-coloured hat was pulled down
over her short pink mane. 'Come on
Rainbow!'

'Or you can all go wild,' said Rainbow.
'That's fine with me, too.'

Everypony watched as Rainbow Dash
parted the crowd with her confident trot
and took her place next to Pinkie Pie.

The board had lines where ponies could write their names and dares, and a spot for a check mark if Rainbow completed the dare successfully. Even though she hadn't read any of the dares yet, Rainbow had no doubt that every row would have a check mark next to it soon. She was fearless. Just like her hero, Daring Do!

'Thanks for coming!' Rainbow shouted to the crowd. 'I'm pretty excited to see you all!' She took notice of Twilight, Rarity, Fluttershy and Applejack entering the square. They all had funny

looks on their faces. What was the big deal? She was just trying to prove how brave she was.

'Pssst, Pinkie, will you do the honours of

reading the first dare?' whispered Rainbow Dash. 'It looks cooler if I have an assistant.'

'Sure thing, Rainbow!' Pinkie chirped, and faced the crowd. 'Fillies and gentle-colts! The amazing *Daaaaaring Dash* will take on all these extremely difficult challenges to prove that her hero Daring *Do* could also *do* these dares that she will *do*!' Pinkie made a sweeping motion toward the Dash-board. 'Then she will defend her title as Ponyville's most brave, most fearless, most DARING pony!'

The townsponies cheered.

'Daring Dash's first dare is...' Pinkie paused for effect. '... to cross the Ghastly Gorge...'

Rainbow rolled her eyes. That was hardly a challenge.

'On a tightrope...' Pinkie continued,

making a
dramatic face.
'Without using
WINGS! Over the
lair of the quarray
eels!'

'All right!'
Rainbow shouted, flying up into the air.
'Now that's more like it! Everypony follow
me to the gorge!' Rainbow shot off into
the blue sky, leading the way. The crowd
followed, trotting below. Would Rainbow
Dash chicken out and use her wings? Or
would she make a mistake and risk falling

into the jaws of a
giant, scary
quarray eel?!
Twilight,
Applejack and
Fluttershy stuck to

the back of the herd.

'Is this all really necessary?' Twilight asked her friends, walking at an easy pace. 'We all know how brave Rainbow Dash is, but sometimes she takes it a little too far.' Twilight thought of the time Rainbow had become boastful after saving some townsponies and becoming a local hero. Her friends had devised a plan to remind her to keep her hooves on the ground. Clearly, that lesson was beginning to wear off.

'Don't you fret, sugarcube!' Applejack reassured her. 'I reckon she'll do a couple of dares and it'll all be over in two shakes of a filly's tail. Now come on!'

Rarity trotted
up to them.
'If anypony
understands the
allure of
attention, it's me.
But somepony

ought to tell her that if she's going to be
famous, she should look the part. A
costume would really add a certain
something.'

'Rarity, I don't think that would do
much to discourage the whole thing,'
scolded Twilight.

'I was just *saying*,' Rarity huffed.

Up front, Rainbow was doubling back through the crowd, hoof-bumping anypony she passed. She did a corkscrew flip and flew to the front of the group.

'It looks like she's having fun,' said Fluttershy, walking alongside her friends. 'I just hope she's careful.'

'Me too, Fluttershy,' said Twilight in concern. She watched as Rainbow dived straight towards the ground. At the very last second she did a one-eighty and flew up into the sky, full speed ahead. 'Me too.'

CHAPTER 6
Heating Up

It had been a busy day for Rainbow Dash
and the ponies who had been following
her daring escapades. They'd been all
over Ponyville, watching as she took on
crazy challenges. Some were thrilling – like
when Snips and Snails had dared her to
swim to the bottom of the disgusting

swamp, Froggy Bottom
Bogg. Rainbow had got
completely covered in
green slime!

Others were not
quite *as* exciting –
like Pinkie's dare for
Rainbow to babysit her
favourite yellow
balloon for an hour. ('So many
things could happen if he's left alone!'
she'd insisted.) But still, Rainbow Dash
had completed each and every task, no
matter the level of difficulty.

Rainbow took off into the air and felt
the cool rush of the wind in her mane.
'What else have you got for me?!' she
shouted to the ponies below.

There was only about an hour left of
daylight before Princess Luna would be

lowering the moon over Equestria. But that was more than enough time to get a few more dares in. Rainbow Dash's friends were getting more and more worried. She'd proved her point; why didn't Rainbow just stop?

'What was it you said?' Twilight turned to Applejack. 'Just a few dares and she'll be done? Look at her – she's been doing daring things like Daring Do all day!'

Applejack shrugged. 'Maybe we can try a different approach to get her to give it up.' She trotted up to Pinkie and whispered something in her ear. Pinkie nodded and scribbled a new dare on the board.

Rainbow Dash landed and trotted to the middle of the dwindling crowd.

'Pinkie Pie, let's go over all the amazing feats I have completed so far.'

'Oooh, fun idea!' Pinkie said, turning  to the Daring Dash-board. She pointed to each item with a long, glittery wand. 'First, you tightrope-walked across quarray eel dwellings at Ghastly Gorge with no wings.'

The crowd murmured their approval.

'Piece of apple cake!' said Rainbow, hoof-bumping a nearby stallion.

'Then, you went inside the scary, old abandoned barn filled with bats...'

'I wasn't scared for a single second!' Rainbow assured her fans. 'If anything, those bats were afraid of *me*.'

'Awww,' said Fluttershy, thinking of the

poor little bats. 'I hope they're OK.'

'Then...' Pinkie took a long, deep breath and said very fast, '...you swam in the bogg, babysat my balloon, spun around in a circle two hundred times, gave Rarity's kitty-cat, Opal, a bath, knocked on Cranky Doodle Donkey's door during his bridge game, performed a Sonic Rainboom through the tree obstacle course at Sweet Apple Acres, and now you're about to eat the hottest chilli peppers in all of Equestria!'

'Woo-hoo!' Rainbow smiled. Then the last part registered. 'Wait – did you say something about chilli peppers?' Rainbow disliked hot peppers more than any other food. And there was only one pony she'd told that secret to: Applejack!

'Yeah, she sure did,' said the yellow country pony, stepping forward. 'Peppers from South Amareica. I just got some down at the Fillydelphia market last week. The pony who sold 'em to me carried them across the San Palomino Desert. He said a couple of those guys around the orchard would keep out pesky pests,' Applejack explained. She looked Rainbow Dash straight in the eyes. 'He also said that one lil' bite of one of 'em would make fire shoot out yer ears.'

'TO THE BARN!' shouted Pinkie Pie, bouncing up and down. 'Let's get the fire peppers!'

'But…but…' Rainbow Dash began to protest. Beads of sweat started to form on her forehead. 'I don't like—'

'Yeeeeah?' said Applejack, giving a little wink to her friends. Twilight looked hopeful. Maybe her plan to get Rainbow to quit all this darepony stuff might just work. There was no way Rainbow Dash would ever eat a chilli pepper.

Rainbow looked around at her audience. It was like they knew she was about to be defeated by some tiny, little, itty-bitty hot peppers. But that couldn't happen! Not now, after she'd done all that other stuff.

'What I *meant* was ...' Rainbow forced herself to stand a little taller. 'I don't like how long you're taking to give me those peppers!' She smiled nervously. That seemed to satisfy the onlookers.

'What?!' replied Applejack. 'Are you sure? Well, colour me surprised and call me Golden Russet!' Applejack felt a little silly now that her plan was going to backfire.

'She's going to do it!' a

yellow Pegasus with a blue mane shouted.

'Go, Rainbow!' added Sweetie Drops.
'Rain-bow! Rain-bow!' she chanted. The
whole crowd was joining in.

'That didn't go quite as planned,'
Applejack admitted to Twilight.
Apparently, Rainbow Dash was on a roll,
and she wasn't going to cool it for just
anything. Not even a hot, hot pepper.

★　★　★

As soon as Rainbow Dash bit into the
pepper, weird things started to happen.
First, she felt like her mouth was on fire.
Then, she could have sworn she saw
Daring Do herself in the crowd. Finally,
her ears began to feel hot and she heard
the booming laughter of Ahuizotl telling

her she could never defeat him.

Rainbow coughed, and a few multi-coloured flames burst out.

'Look at that!' Spike clapped his claws together. 'Rainbow can send all the letters  to Princess Celestia now!' He was usually the only one who could breathe fire, as well as use its magic to deliver messages across Equestria.

'All right, now. Drink up, sugarcube!' Applejack patted Rainbow Dash on the back. She had brought Rainbow an endless supply of water and apple juice to calm her tongue. She felt very guilty about challenging Rainbow. Her plan had gone up in smoke.

'Thanks,' said Rainbow, taking a big gulp.

'I've never seen anything like that.'
Fluttershy shook her head in disbelief.

'Your face turned as red as an apple!'
added Applejack.

'What about those rainbow flames
that were shooting out of your ears?!'
Pinkie squealed.

Rainbow groaned, sipping from her
cup. 'At least it impressed everypony,
because those peppers were brutal!'

Twilight gave Rainbow a stern look.
'That's what we're worried about. Your
daring ways are putting you in danger!'

Rarity, Fluttershy and Applejack all
looked at Rainbow in concern. Pinkie
slumped down with the realisation that
she'd been encouraging her all along.

'What?' Rainbow Dash took another
sip of juice. 'I'm totally good. And plus, I
thrive on danger.'

'Rainbow, my dear,' Rarity chimed in.
'What she's *trying* to say is that nopony
expects you to be as brave as Daring Do.
Maybe you should just focus on being
Rainbow Dash. Hmm?' Rarity batted
her long eyelashes and swished her
purple mane.

'As nice as that is, guys, I think
I'll stick to being the bravest pony in
town.' Rainbow trotted to the door. 'But
thanks for all the juice! Now I'm ready for
more action.'

'I liked this whole Daring Do thing better when it was just about reading books,' said Twilight with a sigh.

CHAPTER 7
Talk of the Town

The next morning, Rainbow Dash awoke to the sound of a loud thunderclap. She popped her head out of the window of her home in Cloudsdale. The other Pegasi were darting around and jumping on the thick, grey clouds to drain them. With each push, big raindrops fell on the landscape below. It was pouring!

'That's funny,' said Rainbow Dash, still a little groggy. 'I don't remember a thunderstorm being scheduled for today.' Usually, Rainbow Dash knew when all the weather changes were supposed to happen.

Glitter Dew, a purple Pegasus with a blue mane and a starry cloud for a cutie mark, heard her and flew over. 'We changed the schedule yesterday, but nopony could find you!'

'What was I doing yesterday that was so important that I'd miss the weather schedule?' asked Rainbow Dash, scratching her head. Her brain felt a bit fuzzy. She'd had a weird dream about walking on a tightrope and eating hot peppers. Unless… that was real! Rainbow touched her hoof to her mouth. Her tongue still felt a little numb.

The events of the previous day came flooding back to her. 'That was no dream – that *is* what I was doing!' she said aloud. Rainbow Dash had spent all day zipping around Ponyville, showing everypony that she was the bravest pony ever. Now, she was known as Daring Dash! 'Great job, me!' she said, patting herself on the back with her right wing.

Suddenly, Rainbow Dash couldn't wait a single second longer to get down to Ponyville to greet everypony. Even though Twilight, Applejack, Rarity and Fluttershy had been totally sceptical before, they'd have to admit that she kicked serious flank on those dares and nothing bad had happened! They really could be such a group of worry-ponies. All Rainbow Dash had to do now was wait for their apologies. And in the meantime, she would enjoy the praise that came with the title of being Ponyville's bravest.

'Sorry, guys,' Rainbow shouted to the other Pegasi. 'I've got somewhere to be!' Rainbow stretched her blue wings and smoothed down her multicoloured mane. She gave herself a quick wink in the mirror and took off for Ponyville below.

Rainbow soared down from the sky and immediately noticed how full the town square looked. Apparently, word of Daring Dash's amazing feats had been spread across Ponyville by Wild Fire. There were twice as many fans as yesterday. They were excitedly recapping their favourite dares. Some of them were even wearing their Daring Do costumes from the book party, but had added rainbow-coloured wigs to the look.

Wow, thought Rainbow. *There sure are a lot of ponies here to see me.*

'Are you all excited for Daring Dash?!' Pinkie Pie shouted to the herd. She was standing on the platform in front of the Dash-board. Her outfit of choice was a rainbow-coloured 'Daring Dash' T-shirt and a hat that looked like a giant hot chilli pepper.

For some strange reason, Rainbow was starting to feel a little bit panicked. It was confusing. The scene certainly had a ton of things she loved – a crowd cheering her name, her best friends watching, and new, thrilling challenges to take on. Maybe it would be better to keep her entrance low-key this time. She landed in an alleyway and crept onto the scene, unnoticed.

A few more ponies trotted up, and Rainbow quickly darted behind a shop to listen to the conversation.

'I'm going to dare Daring Dash to hoof-wrestle with Snowflake – the strongest Pegasus in Cloudsdale!' said a pink pony with a curly teal mane.

'Well, I'm going to dare her to fight a manticore!' added an orange Unicorn with a cactus cutie mark. 'With her bare hooves!'

'How about daring her to get a hooficure?' suggested their purple Earth Pony pal with a giggle. Rainbow cringed.

If there was anything she hated more than chilli peppers, it was beauty treatments at the Ponyville Day Spa.

'Ooh, a hooficure?!' whispered Pinkie into Rainbow's ear. 'How are you going to do that? You hate the Spa!'

'Whoa! Where'd you come from?' shouted Rainbow, jumping back in shock and landing in the town square. Rainbow looked up at the platform in confusion.

'Is something wrong?' said Fluttershy, floating down to meet the two of them. 'You seem a little jumpy today, Rainbow.'

'Of course not!' Rainbow shot back. 'Everything is perfect!' She took off towards the stage, leaving a rainbow trail behind her. But as she landed, a mass of dark clouds began to drift over the square. Then a bright shock of light zigzagged across the sky. Rain poured down and began to drench the ponies.

'Aw, come on, guys!' Rainbow shouted up at the sky. 'Couldn't you wait just a little longer to do that? We are sort of in the middle of something here.'

'Sorry, Rainbow Dash!' Silverstream, a grey Pegasus with a blue mane, shouted. 'Carry on!'

'Thank you!' she shouted back. Even the Pegasi did what she said.

Finally the clouds parted, and a strong ray of sunlight pierced through onto the crowd. One spot was immediately lit up, drawing everypony's attention.

Standing in the middle was none other than Zecora – Ponyville's resident shaman! She wore lots of gold necklaces and a set of shimmering hoops in her ears. Her left foreleg was adorned with shiny bangles and  she wore her black-and-white-striped mane short.

'What's up, Zecora?' said Rainbow Dash casually. She was a little nervous about the worried look on Zecora's face, but Rainbow couldn't let anypony see that. Zecora had a taste for the dramatic, and the whole clouds parting, personal-spotlight business had not helped the situation. Maybe whatever Zecora had to say would be no big deal.

'Citizens of Ponyville!' she bellowed in her rich, deep voice. Zecora paused, like she was struggling to find her strength.

'Is everything OK?' Twilight stepped forward, her voice doing little to hide her alarm.

Zecora continued, 'I've come to summon the pony who has proved bravest…'

'Oh, well, in that case, you're looking for me. Bravest pony in town right here.' Rainbow pointed to herself and puffed up with pride.

'…for only she can be the one to save us!'

On the other hoof, maybe it *was* time to panic.

Zecora's gold hoop earrings glistened as she nodded her head. 'Of course,

Rainbow Dash should be the one! Her skills and courage are second to none.'

The zebra made her way towards the platform. A few ponies jumped out of the way, scared. It was silly. Rainbow Dash and her friends knew that Zecora wasn't actually an evil enchantress like they'd originally thought. She may have been lots of things – mystical, magical, and mysterious – but evil was definitely not one of them.

'Anything you need, Daring Dash will do,' Rainbow assured her with a salute. 'So...uh, what is it I'm doing?'

Zecora looked round at the group of ponies, her blue eyes full of worry.
'A token that provides us with protection was stolen for another's collection.'

'OK,' Rainbow Dash nodded. 'So you're saying it's pretty important and stuff. Got it. What is it?'

'The precious relic of a golden hue resembles the hook of a horse's shoe.' Zecora waved her hoof towards the crowd, and a three-dimensional image of the relic appeared out of wispy green smoke. It spun around slowly in the air. One side of the horseshoe was completely gold, and the reverse looked rusted.

Twilight Sparkle gasped and stepped forward. 'You couldn't possibly mean . . . the Half-gilded Horseshoe?!'

Rainbow Dash looked around to see if anypony else knew what Twilight was talking about, but their faces were all blank. Twilight knew a lot from all her studies on magical history.

'The what?'
Applejack cocked her
head to the side.

'Did she just say
something about *gilded*
shoes?' Rarity trilled.
'Now you've got my attention!'

'It's not *really* a shoe, the Half-gilded
Horseshoe is like a key of sorts. To the
Spirit Circle,' Twilight explained. 'The
myth says that the pony who unlocks it
will find a room full of treasures, but at a
great cost.'

'Treasures?' asked Spike, his eyes
sparkling. 'Like gems? Big ones?'

'Maybe . . . but nopony really knows,'
said Twilight. 'Honestly, I really thought
the whole thing was an old pony's tale.'

'Much of the legend is a mystery, and
most regard it as ancient history,' said

Zecora. 'But, I have failed as the key's protector, and so must prepare to face these spectres.'

'Am I missing something here?' Rainbow Dash asked. 'An old rusty shoe was stolen and now somepony's going to score some treasure. And this puts us in danger how?'

Zecora swatted away the green smoke with her hoof. 'The ghosts will be free when key meets lock. If you want to save

Ponyville, fly fast, don't walk!'

Rainbow wasn't too sure about legends or ghosts, but if there was one thing she knew, it was flying fast. She stepped forward. 'I'll do it!'

The shaman sighed and patted

Rainbow on the shoulder. 'It is a great relief that our best flyer will be the one to put out this fire.'

'You bet! Never fear, Ponyville. Daring Dash is here!' she shouted. Finally, she had her own real book-worthy adventure to star in!

CHAPTER 8
Well Suited

The carousel boutique was a mess. Swatches of green fabric lay on every surface, and thread and ribbons littered the floor. Half-drunk cups of tea sat on the sewing table.

Rarity paced around Rainbow Dash, deep in concentration. 'Stretch your left

wing out again, please. And stop moving so much.'

Rainbow sighed and did as she was told. Standing still was the worst.

'I don't see why you need to add anything to it,' groaned Rainbow. 'My Daring Do costume from Nightmare Night is totally fine for my quest to recover the Half-gilded Horseshoe.' She looked at herself in the full-length mirror. With her green shirt and helmet on, Rainbow was the spitting image of her hero. Well, almost.

'Because I *insist*,' Rarity said. 'If you're not going to let any of us go with you, you have to at least let your friends help you prepare. You are seriously lacking in utility pockets.'

'You know, Rainbow,' Applejack chimed in. 'You can still change your mind. We'll all be ready to go with you in a jiffy – just say the word.'

Fluttershy, Pinkie Pie and Twilight nodded.

'Yeah! It'll be like a party!' Pinkie Pie added. 'But instead of streamers and balloons, there will be scary beasts and spiky hedges! And I'll bring cupcakes. There's always room for cupcakes.'

'Thanks, guys,' Rainbow replied. 'But

if I'm going to maintain my image as the fastest and bravest, I can't have other ponies slowing me down. Nothing personal.'

'In that case, we better go over my research on the Spirit Circle.' Twilight used her horn to magically carry over a big stack of books. They landed with a thud. 'I think you'll be interested in what I discovered.'

★　★　✶

'So let me get this straight...' said Rainbow. She was looking through one of the Daring Do books, hoping to memorise some cool moves. 'The entrance to the Spirit Circle can be found by...'

Twilight sighed. They had been over this already. She was trying to make sure Rainbow knew everything that she had found, but the Pegasus wasn't making it easy. 'By the Dual Stronghold – whatever that is – and is only visible once every five seasons... on the seventh day of the... third week of the year.'

'That's so random,' Rainbow said coolly, flipping a page in her book.

'It's tomorrow!' Twilight pointed to the calendar on her wall. 'Whoever took the Half-gilded Horseshoe will be there, waiting for the entrance to appear.'

'Well, I'll be ready with the move that Daring Do used in the final scene of book four – the old switch 'n' fly. This is going to be totally easy!' Rainbow said.

She pictured getting to the entrance of the Spirit Circle just in the nick of time.

Then she would distract the Half-gilded Horseshoe thief with an awesome stunt, snatch the relic by switching it with an item of equal weight and size, and zoom off into the sky to return it safely to Zecora. She would be miles above the thief by the time he noticed what had happened.

'Rainbow, don't forget the most important part,' warned Twilight. 'If whoever took the Half-gilded Horseshoe opens the entrance, the spirits will get out!'

'Yeah, yeah,' Rainbow Dash replied. She was already wondering if Mayor Mare would give her a medal.

Twilight came up close to Rainbow Dash and tried to look her in the eye. 'And if they do, they will be freed for another whole season. You have to

make sure the entrance is closed!
Don't let the spirits out!'

'Yeah, got it…' Rainbow answered.
'Closed and stuff.' But Rainbow Dash's
head was still in the clouds.

CHAPTER 9
Enter the Everfree

The six ponies, Zecora and Spike all stood at the clearing that led to the Everfree Forest. Rainbow Dash was wearing her new costume that, thanks to Rarity, had plenty of new pockets and a matching lightweight saddlebag. A picture of her cutie mark – a cloud with a rainbow lightning bolt – was embroidered on her shirt, and the fabric on her helmet was rainbow-coloured. She looked the part. Now it was all up to her.

'You sure you don't want company?' asked Applejack. 'I feel mighty funny sending you out there alone.' They had been to the Everfree Forest more times than Applejack had liked, but at least they'd been together. It was a spooky place.

'*No*,' Rainbow answered. 'Being the bravest means you don't need help.'

'Everypony needs help sometimes,' offered Fluttershy.

'I know I do,' Applejack insisted. 'Remember when I tried to buck all the

trees in Sweet Apple Acres on my own?'

Zecora bowed her head. 'It is time, Rainbow Dash, and I hope you are ready. May your wing beats be strong and your hoof beats be steady.'

'Thanks. And don't worry, Zecora,' said Rainbow. 'I'll have the Half-gilded Horseshoe back in no time. No ghosts will haunt Ponyville if Daring Dash has anything to say about it.' Rainbow twisted into an action pose – right arm up to the sky, wings spread out.

Zecora looked slightly reassured.

Rainbow Dash gulped and took a step forward. 'See ya later, everypony.'

'Wait!' shouted Twilight Sparkle. 'We didn't even get to show you your tools yet.'

'My what?' said Rainbow, impatiently.

'Each of those new pockets has a little something from one of us to help you on your way,' explained Rarity, smiling warmly. 'Go ahead and look.'

Rainbow Dash emptied the pockets to find a piece of rope from Applejack, a mini teddy bear from Fluttershy, some green cupcakes (and one pink one) from Pinkie Pie, a pair of horseshoes from Rarity, and a Sapphire Stone bookmark from Twilight. They were the weirdest adventure 'tools' she'd ever seen. She wasn't sure how any of these things was

going to help her, but it was a nice gesture, so Rainbow played along. 'I told you there was always room for cupcakes!' squealed Pinkie Pie. 'The pink one's for you.'

'Thanks,' said Rainbow, who was

planning to ditch the items as soon as she
was out of sight. No need to have
anything extra weighing her down – that
went for extra ponies *and* gifts. She stuffed
the presents back in her pockets. 'Now

I'm off for real!' Rainbow announced.
Then she flapped her wings and soared
straight towards her destiny.

As soon as Rainbow Dash was out of
sight, Twilight turned to the
other girls. 'Are you all ready
to go?'

'Yes!' Applejack, Fluttershy,
Rarity and Pinkie Pie said

together.

Zecora bowed to them and Spike gave a little wave. 'Be careful out there! Good luck!' the dragon said as the five ponies trotted towards the dangerous forest. He was pretty sure they were going to need it.

CHAPTER 10
In the Thick of It

Rainbow Dash took a deep breath as she flew off. It was a hot day, and the sun hung low in the sky. The gentle light illuminated every rock, tree and bramble on the edge of the Everfree Forest. It was serene, but it was a false sense of calm. In a second, Rainbow would be deep inside it – the most wild, unpredictable place in all of Equestria. Other than Pinkie Pie's head, of course.

Exotic birds cried out from the treetops. They seemed almost like they were saying, 'Do Not Enter!' but there was no way Daring Dash was going to heed the warning. She was the bravest pony in town. And she was on a mission to save Ponyville. Now where to start? Rainbow Dash looked around and surveyed her options.

There was no visible path up ahead. Every direction was dense with green foliage that seemed to fade into black. It looked so . . . dark and cold. Rainbow Dash shuddered but then quickly shook off her doubt.

'I can *totally* do this. I'm Daring Dash!' she said out loud to nopony. She started to realise just how alone she was.

Suddenly, the sound of deep, booming laughter echoed through the trees. It sent shivers up Rainbow's spine. She told herself it was just a trick of her mind. She had to keep moving.

Fifteen minutes later, however, Rainbow Dash hadn't got any further. When she  saw the same purple tree with gnarly roots, she knew she had been flying in a giant circle! She needed a better plan if she was ever going to find the entrance to the Spirit Circle before the relic thief.

Rainbow found a safe spot and landed. She hadn't heard the scary laugh again and there had been no signs of anypony else. Something told her that it wouldn't stay that way for long.

'Now where did I put that map?' Rainbow said to herself as she riffled through her bag. 'I know it's in here somewhere.'

Rarity's pair of shoes clanked together and squished into one of the green cupcakes. What had her friends been thinking?

'Yuck!' Rainbow took one of the shoes and flung it behind her. She expected to hear a thud, but instead she noticed a low gurgling noise, followed by a loud *SNAP*! It sounded like a huge set of teeth.

Rainbow Dash got the funny feeling that she wasn't alone any more. She turned around slowly, unsure of what fate had in store for her.

'Ahhh!' Rainbow screamed at a huge pack of Colossa-gators. They had scaly green skin and red eyes and were very different from Pinkie Pie's cute, toothless baby alligator, Gummy, back home.

Rainbow was completely surrounded. She stood frozen in place as they crept towards her. The Colossagators looked very hungry; snapping their massive, sharp-toothed jaws. Did they like to eat ponies? All signs pointed to yes.

Finally, she got hold of herself. Rainbow flew up into the air, but the thick canopy of low-hanging trees prevented her from getting away. She was still within reach of the gators!

'Oh no you don't!' shouted Rainbow, starting to get angry. She flew around,

trying to annoy the giant gators. Maybe if
she could make them dizzy enough,
they'd leave her alone and she could
escape! As she weaved through the tree
trunks, the gators snapped. They
narrowly missed her rainbow tail more
times than she cared to admit.

'Watch this, you ugly gators!' she
yelled, flying as fast as she could around
them. 'That'll teach you to mess with
Daring Dash!' Rainbow landed on the
back of a huge gator to do a little victory
dance. 'Ahhh!' she yelled as the gator
swung around, flinging her into the
branches of a nearby tree.

She tried to take off again, but her tail was stuck! She yanked and pulled, but nothing worked. The biggest gator was getting close. He crawled up slowly, like he was savouring his victory. If she didn't break free soon, he would be savouring his lunch – a rainbow Pegasus!

Rainbow looked around for something, *anything* to throw at him. She reached into her saddlebag and grabbed the first thing she could find. It was one of Pinkie's green cupcakes. 'If you're so hungry, eat this!' She chucked the cake right into his mouth.

The alligator swallowed the cupcake, burped, and simply walked away. Rainbow couldn't believe her eyes!

What was in those things?! Rainbow reached for another one. It had loopy icing that said the words GATOR CUPCAKE on it. She threw another at a different gator. The same thing happened. They were . . . gator treats!

'Pinkie Pie, you're a genius!' Rainbow shouted into the air.

Pinkie popped her head out of a nearby tree. 'Awww, thanks, Rainbow!'

Luckily, Rainbow was so caught up in the action that she didn't notice her friend almost blow the cover of the other ponies. Rainbow wasn't supposed to know that they were following her. That would ruin the plan!

After Rainbow had got rid of all the alligators, she only had one cupcake left. It was the pink one, so she ate it. She

hadn't even realised how hungry
she was. She guessed Pinkie was
right about the whole 'making
room for cupcakes' thing.

It was a minor victory. Even if
she was no closer to finding the
Half-gilded Horseshoe, at least a giant
creature wasn't eating her for lunch right
now. But Rainbow needed to buckle
down if she was going to make it to the
Spirit Circle by nightfall.

It would help if she had some idea
where she was going.

Rainbow finally found her map of
Equestria and
began to search for
a sign of a Dual
Stronghold. All she
could see beyond
the forest were

castle ruins. Rainbow suddenly found herself wishing that Twilight were there. She would have definitely had an idea about where to find the entrance. Or maybe she already had, and Rainbow just hadn't listened ... Either way, it was too late now.

Rainbow rolled up her map and soldiered on into the unknown.

CHAPTER 11
A Sinking Feeling

There was a hint of something glowing
and red in the distance. Rainbow watched
with curiosity as it drifted and swirled
through the branches before escaping
behind a large bush. It looked like the
green magic smoke Zecora had used to
show them the Half-gilded Horseshoe.

Maybe she was on the right track!

She took off in the direction of the smoke, hoping that it would lead her to the Spirit Circle. 'Hey, wait for me!' shouted Rainbow as she flew along. Soon she'd find the entrance and retrieve the relic, and Ponyville would be safe.

Rainbow reached a large clearing that looked like a lake. But instead of water, the ground was covered with soft white sand. That was strange. Rainbow hadn't seen sand like that anywhere except at the beach or the swimming hole. She had

never seen it in a forest. But the Everfree played by its own mysterious rules. The red smoke hovered over the sand momentarily before disappearing into the woods. Rainbow was about to run after it, when she got a feeling that she shouldn't. She leaped into the air, beating her wings like normal. She soared across the expanse. 'Wait!' she shouted, though she wasn't sure whether smoke could hear anything. She was halfway across when, suddenly, Rainbow felt herself falling! It was as if her wings were frozen in mid-air. She looked down. The sandy ground was approaching fast and there was nothing she could do.

'Rainbooooow!' she heard a voice shout. It sounded like...Applejack?  It had to be the forest playing tricks on her.

Wooompf! Rainbow Dash landed in the sand.

It was a soft cushiony landing. She

found herself slowly sinking into it, so she rested a moment. Then, she reached out her right hoof and pulled her body up. Her hoof disappeared into the pale sand. Rainbow tried her left hoof and the same thing happened. Every step she tried to take brought her deeper into the sinking sand.

'It couldn't be...' Rainbow Dash said aloud, '...quicksand?!'

She tried to spread her wings, but they didn't work. They were still frozen in place by some sort of magic. Now, Rainbow was in up to her knees. If she didn't act fast, the sand would soon swallow her up completely.

'This is probably the only time I will ever say this, but – I wish this would go slower!'

Her words were met with the familiar

sounds of evil laughter, echoing across
the clearing. Rainbow looked around
in desperation for something to grab. The
edge of the sandpit was about ten trots
away. She spotted a sturdy bush
with wiry brambles. If only she had
something to reach it . . . maybe she could
pull herself to safety.

'Applejack's rope!' Rainbow yelled out,
brightening. 'Of course – it's
a lasso!'

Luckily, the sand hadn't
swallowed her saddlebag yet.
She pulled out the lasso,
and pitched it up into the
air with all her might. She
swung it around in a circle like she'd seen
her friend do so many times.

Rainbow Dash tossed the rope at the
shrub. It bounced off the branches and

fell to the ground. 'No!' she shouted, now waist-deep in sand. It was a lot harder than it looked. She made a mental note to compliment Applejack on her lasso skills when she got home. *If* she got home.

The thought of never seeing her friends again filled Rainbow with a new resolve. There was no way she was going to let that happen! She pulled the lasso in again and gave it another shot. This time, the loop hooked around the bush.

Rainbow mustered all her strength and pulled. Inch by inch, she reeled herself back to  solid ground. By the time she reached the bush, she was exhausted. She collapsed in a heap. This Pegasus had never been happier to have her hooves firmly on the ground.

CHAPTER 12
Finding Your Place

After what seemed like an eternity of trotting through the forest, Rainbow finally stopped. She had no leads on how to find the Dual Stronghold or the Spirit Circle. She was beginning to wonder if they even existed.

'Dual Stronghold…' Rainbow Dash said

out loud, sitting on a mossy log. '*Dual* means 'two', so ... two stronghold?'

She scratched her head. What in Equestria was a two stronghold?

It was starting to get dark.

Time was running out, and Rainbow was starting to feel very alone. She wondered what her friends were doing. Applejack was probably having dinner with Apple Bloom, Big Mac and Granny Smith. Maybe Fluttershy was reading Angel Bunny a bedtime story. Twilight might be studying a new spell with Spike. Rarity could have been designing dresses. And Pinkie Pie was *definitely* baking a giant cake to pop out of – just for fun.

All those things sounded better than being stranded in a scary forest on an aimless mission. Rainbow grabbed Fluttershy's teddy bear and curled up into a ball. She started to drift off when she heard a voice softly whispering.

'Don't give up, Daring Dash!' it said. 'You're the bravest pony in Ponyville. You don't want to embarrass yourself, do you?'

'No!' Rainbow sat up and riffled through her saddlebag for her map. She pulled out the Sapphire Stone bookmark that Twilight had given her and stared at it. Why this instead of something useful like Applejack's lasso or Pinkie Pie's cupcakes? Twilight was usually the most practical one. Her gift didn't make sense.

'I wish this was over!' Rainbow shouted, throwing the bookmark on the ground. She looked down at it. 'I wish I was with my friends,' she whimpered, picking it up and holding it close. Why had she pushed them away? If they were here, this would have been so much easier.

'I wish . . . I were at the Dual Stronghold right now!'

And suddenly, a bright white light blinded Rainbow.

She blinked and rubbed her eyes with her hoof. When she regained her sight, she saw that she had been magically transported! Sneaky Twilight had given her an enchanted bookmark! Instead of being surrounded by dark trees and low-hanging vines, Rainbow found herself in front of a large, crumbling stone structure. She knew this place!

'The Castle of the Two Sisters!' she exclaimed. So that's what *Dual Stronghold* was code for. *Stronghold* was just a fancy word for 'castle'. If she had figured that out sooner, she could have saved herself a lot of time and trouble. But there was no time for regrets now. The Spirit Circle had to be nearby. Rainbow could feel it.

She took off towards the castle. A puff of the swirling red smoke was just ahead. 'Aha! I see you!' Rainbow shouted in triumph, flying after it. It led her through a maze of corridors and staircases that she didn't even know existed. Finally, she ran out into a grassy clearing. The smoke joined a massive cloud and spun like a slow, red tornado.

'Rainbow Dash!' a voice cried out. 'She's here!'

'Don't worry about us!' cried another. 'Close the entrance!'

'Fluttershy? Twilight? Is that you?' Rainbow would recognise her friends' voices anywhere. They sounded like they were in trouble, but where were they?

'Finally, Daring Dash has arrived!'
a deep voice bellowed. 'I wasn't sure if you
had survived.'

A figure stepped forward but was still
shrouded in red smoke. The dark outline
heaved with laughter, and a shiver went
up Rainbow Dash's spine. It was the same
laugh she had been hearing all along.

'Show yourself, you ... you ... *coward*!'
Rainbow squeaked.

'Prepare yourself to be amazed!' the
voice cackled. The red smoke parted and
out stepped a massive zebra. 'For you are
graced by the presence of Braze!'

He had blood-red eyes and an earring
made of orange-and-yellow phoenix
feathers. He had stripes just like Zecora,
only his weren't black-and-white; they
were red, orange and yellow and looked
like flames of fire. It was a bit scary.

'I'm not afraid of you, Braze!' Rainbow Dash lied. 'Who are you and what have you done with my friends?!'

Braze slowly walked up to Rainbow. He looked down at her with a wicked smile. 'I knew they would be useful in this endeavour. Open the door, or they're mine for ever!' He made a sweeping

motion with his hoof to reveal Twilight, Applejack, Fluttershy, Rarity and Pinkie Pie all tied together with a magical red fire-rope. They were all wearing helmets and shirts just like hers.

Rainbow gasped and flew over to them. 'What are you doing here?!'

'We're sorry
for following
you, Rainbow,'
Applejack said.
'Honest. We just
wanted to make sure you
were safe!'

'We tried to let you have your
adventure...' Fluttershy added. 'But...'

'But then this big meanie zebra caught
us and brought us here!' Pinkie Pie
pouted, squirming around. Her mane
was messier than usual, poking out of her
helmet, and she had painted lines across
her cheeks like a warrior. 'And we're all
out of cupcakes.' Her stomach grumbled
loudly. 'Which is the worst part!'

'This fire-rope is frying my mane!'
Rarity cried, touching her purple locks.

'Don't worry, guys! I'll have you free in

a second.' Rainbow reached for the fiery rope, but it burned her hoof. 'Ouch!'

Braze laughed. 'Did you really think I'd make it that easy? Come here, Daring Dash, this choice will be breezy!' The zebra waved his hoof, and Rainbow found herself being dragged towards him. He turned her around to face a large, freestanding stone door.

It had all sorts of ancient pony carvings across it that seemed to tell a story. There was a Pegasus, who looked like Rainbow Dash, soaring through the

clouds with a striped trail behind her. The paint had worn off, but it could have been a rainbow. In the middle was a U-shaped slot. Perfect for a horseshoe. The Half-gilded Horseshoe. The key that could unleash all the scary spirits into Ponyville.

She hated to admit it, but Rainbow was actually nervous. 'Hand over the horseshoe, Braze!' she demanded, trying to hide her nerves. 'And release my friends! This is between you...and me!' She stood taller and gritted her teeth. Nopony, or zebra, was going to mess with her friends.

Braze nodded his head, his feather earring swishing back and forth. 'Yes, dear Dash, *you* are what I need! It's the only way for your friends to be freed. The spirits will only open the room for the one who can do a Sonic Rainboom.'

He tossed the Half-gilded Horseshoe into the air to show off. It twirled just as it

had in Zecora's green flames. As it
sparkled in the light, Rainbow noticed
that the edge caught one of the fire-
ropes, cutting it slightly. It gave Rainbow
an idea.

'You want me to open the door to the
Spirit Circle for you?' Rainbow asked,
playing along. 'And then you'll untie your
fire-rope and let my friends go?'

Braze circled her, little flames
escaping from his hooves with each step.
'Yes! Then I'll disappear with my
treasure, and you can leave at your
leisure.' He smirked.

'Deal!' Rainbow nodded. A look of
horror flashed across Twilight Sparkle's
face. Clearly, she thought it was a trick.
But Rainbow had a plan.

'Look at that! Aren't you clever? Now
insert the key and pull the lever!' Braze

rubbed his hooves together greedily. He tossed Rainbow the Half-gilded Horseshoe. The ponies held their breath as Rainbow caught it. Was she really going to open the door and let the spirits out?

If only she could distract Braze somehow...

Rainbow gave a sly wink, and Pinkie Pie seemed to get the hint. 'Hey, Mr Braaaaaaze?' she chirped. 'Do you have any snacks?! I'm sooo hungry!'

Braze turned around and growled in rage. 'I know nothing of your pony diet! Stop talking for once and just be quiet!'

It had been just enough time for Rainbow to make the switch and slip the

Half-gilded Horseshoe into her bag.

'One haunted room full of treasure, coming right up!' Rainbow said, inserting a regular horseshoe, the gift from Rarity, into the slot. She slowly pulled the lever down.

CHAPTER 13
Dash to Safety

'Guess you were wrong!' Rainbow shrugged as she pushed down on the lever again. 'It doesn't work.' Her plan was going even better than expected. Braze hadn't noticed the horseshoe had been switched.

'No! No! This cannot be!' Braze

looked towards the sky and let out a deep, angry growl. 'I have secured both the Pegasus and the key!'

'Maybe you should just let us go and git along now, Braze,' Applejack shouted, struggling against the fire-rope. 'Looks like you won't be openin' any spooky doors today.'

'Give it up, Braze!' shouted Twilight. 'The entrance is going to close any minute and you've got nothing.'

'No!' Braze shouted, and began to pace back and forth. He started mumbling to himself, presumably in rhymes. It was the perfect time for Rainbow to make her move. She crept over to her friends, careful not to let Braze see what she was pulling out of her bag...

'The Half-gilded Horseshoe!' Twilight exclaimed. 'It's been in your bag this whole time?'

'What?!' Braze galloped over and stood between Rainbow and her friends. 'I knew that you were being phoney! Give it back now, you deceitful pony!'

Rainbow Dash could see that the door was starting to lower into the ground. She just had to buy enough time to keep the Half-gilded Horseshoe away from him until it was gone. Then, she would cut her friends free and they could escape!

'I'll never surrender it to you, Braze!' Rainbow shouted. She shot up into the air just as Braze threw a fire-rope at her. It singed the bottom of her tail. Rainbow dived back towards her friends, hoping to cut the rope, but Braze was in the way. He reached out for the horseshoe and almost got it.

"Hey, Braze! Watch this!" Rainbow hollered. She held the horseshoe up and narrowed her eyes to aim. Then, she flung it like a boomerang – right at her Ponyville friends!

Braze dived for it.

The shoe flew through the air, landing in position to slice through the fire-rope. It doubled back to Rainbow, as if it were

under her control. She caught it and blew the residual smoke off its surface. She put it safely away

and gave her bag a pat. The ponies broke
free and cheered.

'All right!' Pinkie Pie
squealed, jumping up
and down. 'Wahooo!'

'You did it!' said
Fluttershy.

'Thank you, darling,'
said Rarity, smoothing down her purple
mane.

'Now let's get out of here,' said
Rainbow. 'This dude is creeping me out.'

Braze was standing over the door,
which had only a few inches left above
ground. He was shaking his head with a
pained expression on his face. Finally, the
door was sucked into the earth. Now,
there was just grass. He let out a sob.

'You may have won this time, Daring
Dash..." Braze looked at Rainbow, his

eyes aflame. "But I will be back to claim my stash! And when the door is back anew...I will not stop till I find you!"

Braze cackled and vanished into a burst of flames.

"And I'll be ready for him," said Rainbow. She wasn't going to let some greedy zebra put her friends or her town in danger again. But maybe next time, she would agree to some help. She smiled at her friends.

"I mean – *we'll* be ready for him."

"And so, with Braze defeated and the Half-Gilded Horseshoe secured..." said Twilight, quoting a famous line from the Daring Do books, "Ponyville was safe and sound once again, thanks to Daring Dash!'

'...*and* her friends!' said Rainbow Dash proudly. 'Thanks for being there, even when I said you shouldn't be. Plus, I couldn't have done it without those gifts! What was with that bookmark?'

'It's a placeholder,' Twilight blushed. 'I enchanted it to help you find your place.'

'And aren't gator treats the best?' Pinkie Pie sighed. 'Gummy loves them.'

Rainbow laughed. 'You guys really saved my tail.'

'It looks a little burned to me,' commented Rarity. She inspected where the fire-rope had fried it. 'But a trip to Ponyville Day Spa will fix it right up.'

'Anything but that!' cried Rainbow

'And you're supposed to be the brave one?' Twilight joked.

CHAPTER 14
The Bravest Thing

Miss Cheerilee's classroom at the Ponyville Schoolhouse was packed with students from all over the school. The fillies and colts were all buzzing with excitement for today's visitors. The local heroes, Daring Dash and her loyal friends, were going to talk to the class

about their adventure in the Everfree
Forest. All sorts of crazy rumours had
been flying around about exactly what
had happened out there, but today they
were going to set the record straight.

'My big sister
Applejack was
there when
Daring Dash
defeated the
evil zebra,
Braze!' Apple

Bloom bragged to Diamond Tiara, who
turned up her nose.

'And so was mine!'
said Rarity's little
sister, Sweetie
Belle.
'Well, I knew
Rainbow Dash before

she became Daring Dash!' offered Scootaloo, who was wearing her own mini Daring Dash costume.

'All right, let's calm down, my little ponies,' Cheerilee said. 'Let's all give a warm welcome to...Daring Dash!'

'Hey, kids!' Rainbow  trotted in and gave a nervous wave to the students.

Everypony's hooves shot up into the air. They all had questions. But before Rainbow answered any of them, she had something important to say.

'Remember, it may seem cool to be brave and daring – but if there's one thing I learned as Daring Dash, it's that...' Rainbow looked to Rarity,

Applejack, Twilight, Pinkie Pie and Fluttershy, and they all smiled back. '...sometimes the bravest thing a pony can do is accept help from her friends, even when she doesn't think she needs it!'

Rainbow put on her helmet, and the students cheered. 'Now who wants to hear how I was wing-deep in quicksand and used a lasso to pull myself out?!'

Read on for a sneak
peek of the next exciting
MY LITTLE PONY adventure,

Twilight Sparkle and the Spell

All of Equestria had been celebrating since the joyous wedding of Shining Armour and Princess Mi Amore Cadenza – or Cadance, as she was called. The citizens of Equestria, including the newly recovered Crystal Empire, were living in a time of happiness and prosperity. Apples grew in the orchards, creatures big and small played in the lush green fields, and ponies of all three tribes lived in harmony. And now, another promising young royal had joined the highest ranks of pony society. It seemed like the cherry on top of a delicious ice-cream sundae.

Ponies of all kinds from the far reaches of Princess Celestia's kingdom were curious about the new princess who had just been crowned. She was a young Unicorn pony with a violet-hued hide, a beautiful purple-and-pink striped mane, and incredible abilities. Her name was Twilight Sparkle, and she was indeed very special. Stories of her amazing magical gifts had travelled all the way from San Franciscolt to Manehattan. These tales had started to become legendary – especially the one about the time she defeated the evil Queen

Chrysalis in order to save the royal court of Canterlot. All the ponies in Equestria were excited to see what wonders Twilight Sparkle's reign would bring.

Twilight was excited too. Not only did she bear an esteemed new title, but she had received her very own set of wings. *Real* Pegasus wings! She was officially part of a special breed of pony called an Alicorn. This meant that Twilight was now able to harness the magical powers of the Unicorns, the flight abilities of the Pegasi, and the strength of a good, true heart of an Earth Pony.

Read Twilight Sparkle and the Spell to find out what happens next!

Rainbow Dash's Lightning Round

What do you remember from Rainbow Dash's exciting story? Try this quick-fire quiz.

1 What's the name of Rainbow Dash's favourite book series?

a) Daring Do ☐ b) Derring Do ☐ c) Double Do ☐

2 What does Pinkie Pie give to Rainbow Dash to help her on her quest?

a) Muffins ☐ b) Cupcakes ☐ c) Jelly ☐

3 Who dares Rainbow Dash to eat the hottest chilli peppers in Equestria?

a) Twilight Sparkle ☐ b) Fluttershy ☐ c) Applejack ☐

4 Which scary Zebra wants to use the Half-gilded Horseshoe to open the door to the Spirit Circle?

a) Blaze ☐   b) Braze ☐   c) Breeze ☐

5 What is the name of the book club that Twilight Sparkle organises?

a) Golden Oak Library Society ☐   b) Daring Do Bookclub ☐   c) Ponyville Adventure Group ☐

6 Name the pony that runs Ponyville's bookshop.

a) Cliff Hanger ☐   b) Page Turner ☐   c) Plot Twist ☐

Did you get all the questions right?
Check the answers at the bottom of the page.

Pony Profile

Here's everything you need to
know about Rainbow Dash!

Species: Pegasus Pony

Element of Harmony:
Loyalty

Cutie Mark: A rainbow
lightning bolt

Likes: Flying and racing

Dislikes: Not winning
races

Pet: Tank

Rainbow Dash Dots

Join the dots to complete this picture of Rainbow Dash. When you've finished, why not colour it in too!

Match the Ponies' Pets

Do you know whose pet is whose? Match the pony to their pet by drawing a line between them. Check your answers at the bottom of the page.

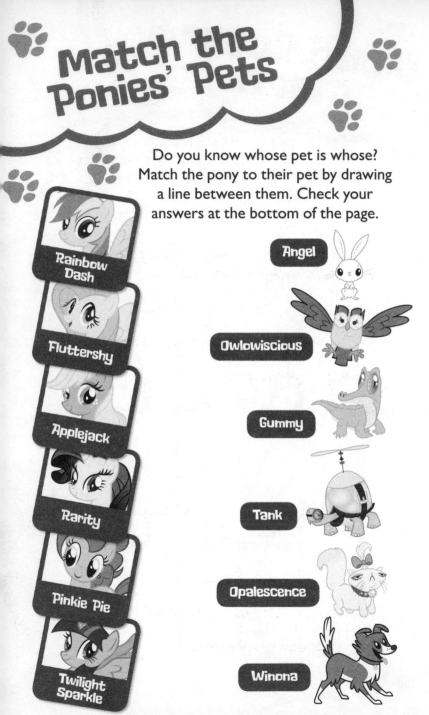

Rainbow Dash

Fluttershy

Applejack

Rarity

Pinkie Pie

Twilight Sparkle

Angel

Owlowiscious

Gummy

Tank

Opalescence

Winona

Cloud Cover Maze

Rainbow Dash is going to see Gilda the Griffon but has got lost in the clouds. Can you help her find her way through and reach Gilda?

Start

Finish

Ponyville Wordsearch

Rainbow Dash is on another mission, to find the names of all her friends in Ponyville in this wordsearch. Can you help her? Words can be forwards, backwards or diagonally.

H	K	J	R	U	S	K	D	O	T	A	N	E	E	Z
G	Q	H	C	H	A	Q	C	A	U	E	T	K	X	U
J	S	I	Z	G	E	L	N	V	F	D	J	Y	F	D
H	Y	V	V	E	J	K	P	A	E	A	W	P	V	N
Q	O	D	Z	C	S	P	G	I	N	Y	L	I	P	I
H	A	S	P	T	E	J	O	C	H	T	A	N	L	E
T	W	I	L	I	G	H	T	S	P	A	R	K	L	E
H	J	D	M	H	Q	E	R	H	R	A	R	I	T	Y
R	T	A	T	V	L	E	H	M	N	Q	F	E	A	H
P	N	J	M	J	T	V	B	S	C	Z	A	P	J	I
H	J	Q	K	T	Z	U	L	Q	F	K	P	I	D	W
F	W	I	U	T	Q	G	N	D	S	G	C	E	N	M
Q	O	L	O	U	H	T	S	R	S	H	Y	D	R	Y
I	F	H	W	R	W	T	C	L	D	V	R	O	A	N
F	O	Q	R	J	U	K	C	A	J	E	L	P	P	A

Twilight Sparkle
Applejack
Fluttershy
Rarity
Pinkie Pie
Tank

Weather Chart

Rainbow Dash and the other Pegasi help to control the weather in Ponyville. But their weather chart has some gaps! Can you fill in what comes next in the sequences?

What's Your Pony Name?

Find out your pony name with this handy guide. Why not work out your friends' pony names too!

Take the first letter of your name:

A – STRAWBERRY

B – DAREDEVIL

C – RAINBOW

D – STARBURST

E – VIOLET

F – SUNSET

G – TULIP

H – REBEL

I – LUNA

J – POPPY

K – RUBY

L – FIRE

M – PEACH

N – FIERCE

O – HAPPY

P – SUNSHINE

Q – BUTTERCUP

R – DISCO

S – DANDELION

T – FUZZY

U – FLASH

V – TWINKLE

W – GIDDY

X – DAYDREAM

Y – BUBBLE

Z – PRANCING

And the month you were born:

January – MOON
February – MANE
March – FLASH
April – BLOSSOM
May – SPRINKLES
June – TAIL
July – PHOENIX
August – WINGS
September – CLOUD
October – BEAM
November – SNOWFLAKE
December – GLITTER

My pony name is:

....

Your Pony

Species:

Cutie Mark:

Likes:

Dislikes:

Pet:

Now you know your pony name, it's time to create your very own pony character. Decorate and colour in the pony on the page, and fill in your own pony profile. Are you a Pegasus, a Unicorn or even an Alicorn? It's up to you!

Double Dash

Can you spot the differences
between the two pictures of
Rainbow Dash below?
There are five to spot!

Fun with Friends

Rainbow Dash loves to spend time with her friends. Here are some ideas for things you can do with yours.

Write your own short story together!

You'll need at least one friend. Simply get a blank piece of paper and start writing the first sentence. When you've finished, pass it on to a friend and when they've finished they pass it back to you or to another friend. Soon you'll have written your own Daring Do mystery!

Throw your very own tea party!

You'll need some friends to come over. Oh and some tea and cakes too!

Have a race!

Get your friends together and head outside to race. Why not ask an adult to time you to see who is the fastest?

Nature trail!

Next time you're outside with your friends, why not jot down what plants, birds and animals you spot. You'll notice nature is everywhere!

Home Sweet Home!

It's time for Rainbow Dash to head home to Cloudiminium. But only one of these paths leads there. Can you show her the way?

A

B

C

Congratulations on completing all these extra special puzzle pages. Even Rainbow Dash is tired out!

See you soon!

Join Twilight Sparkle on her quest to find the Crystal Heart Spell!

OUT NOW